DANDELION SOUL

by

Dona Goldman

Cover designer: Mary Smith Chant
Illustration artist: Mary Smith Chant

Editor: Carol Spelius
Layout editor: Wayne Spelius

LAKE SHORE PUBLISHING
373 Ramsay Road
Deerfield, IL 60015
Phone # (708) 945-4324

ISBN # 0-941363-30-9
copyright 1994
Price: $9.95

FOREWORD

Dona Goldman's depictions of the inherent loneliness and isolation that we all experience at one time or another are almost terrifying in their exactness, but in that loneliness, she also shows us joy, the appreciation of life whether viewing a street below from an apartment, or sitting across the table from a loved one. We are all lonely in our skin, and Ms. Goldman knows that.
Her poems breathe life.

> Walter Griffin
> Atlanta, Georgia.

Former Master-Poet-in-Residence for the Georgia Council for the Arts and Humanities. Author of Western Flyers (1990, University of West Florida) and of poetry published in Harper's, The Atlantic, The Paris Review, Poetry, and The Yale Review.

Table of Contents

DUKE ELLINGTON 1
ALONE WITH THE BIG BANG 2
MICHELANGELO'S *AWAKENING GIANT* 3
OCTOBER DANDELIONS 5
ABOUT VIOLA 6
ACROPOLIS 7
AT A JAZZ CONCERT: THOUGHTS ON IMMORTALITY .. 8
AT DINNER 9
AT THE LAST 10
AUGUST 11

BALLERINA 12
LET ME 13
BETWEEN US LET US STRETCH A STRING 14
BLUEBERRY PICKING 15
PHANTOM 16
A CHILD IS 17
CHRIS 18
DANDELION WINE 19
DANDELIONS 20
DRY LEAVES 21

FATHER 22
THE FIRST WARM WINDY DAY 23
I KNEW AN APPLE TREE 24
HI BLUE 26
IN HONOR OF *TIME* PHOTOGRAPHERS 27
ITALY 28
THE JENNIE ROSE 29
BERGAMO AT SIX O'CLOCK 30
MAHLER SYMPHONY 31
MOM AND DAD 32

MY DOG 33
MY LATEST POEM 34
ONE RAINDROP 35

OPERA AT THE BATHS OF CARACALLA 36
OUR YELLOW 37
CAFE 38
PIAZZA QUIRINALE 39
QUEEN OF THE MOUNTAIN 40
RAIN WHIMSEY 41
SARAJEVO 42

WE TWO 43
SEEKING 45
A SIXTEENTH-NOTE REST 46
RIDING IN THE RAIN 48
THE SIXTH DAY 49
SILENCE 50
A SMOOTH BLACK STONE 51
SNOW-WHITE AND THE SEVEN DWARFS 52
THE THIRTIES: EAST CHICAGO, INDIANA 53
THIS ROSE PETAL 54

TO THE CYNIC AT CHRISTMAS 55
TO YOU, THE RED-HAIRED BOY 56
TOUR GUIDE 57
TRUMP 58
VIEW FROM 175TH STREET 59
TWO TOURISTS MEET 61
WHO? 62
WYOMING EVENING 63
ZELDA 64
IF IT WEREN'T FOR DANDELIONS 65

WISH 66
FOREIGNER 67
AMALFI, ITALY 68
BERGAMO, ITALY 79

DUKE ELLINGTON

Pygmalion moves
in the half light
with his satin doll,
smoothing
in syn-
copated cool
and sophis-
ticated warm
while
mortals keep time.

ALONE WITH THE BIG BANG

I was losing myself
and finding myself
reading my first book
on the history of time,
the big bang and black holes.
They hit my head like a hammer,
the words that said
that a clock at the bottom
of a tower runs slower
than a clock at the top,
but a twin on earth ages faster
than the twin on a long space trip.
My mind stretched up like a cone,
thinner and thinner
than a Hershey kiss at the top,
but infinitely up.
My breath came faster,
heart beat faster.
I wanted to share the universe
but I was alone.
When the telephone rang,
I leaped to answer it,
five leaps for the living room,
four for the dining room,
and snatched up the phone.
It was a wrong number.

MICHELANGELO'S *AWAKENING GIANT*
He was left struggling to free himself
from the block of white marble.
The strong muscles thrust out
from his smooth arm and leg
that have partly escaped
from the chiseled roughness around him,
and agony pushes through his unfinished face.

OCTOBER DANDELIONS

A death cloud above her
moved away only when
she looked away, telling funny stories,
sparkling "hello this is Fanny calling."
Insults to her body   fear   hope
insults   fear   hope   and still
"hello this is Fanny calling."

October last year the death cloud
lowered and she died and also
I think the cloud brought rain.
This year October and rain again
but today I saw dandelions
like fallen stars with jagged leaves.
I never saw dandelions
in October before
"hello this is Fanny calling."

ABOUT VIOLA

Just here I see the stream--
this is all that is needed.
So much is the running
of the here, that start
and solution go unheeded.

Smoothing pebbles, eroding
rocks, always knowing
her course, she reflects the sun
a million-fold,
flickering, reveling, flowing.

ACROPOLIS

Ancient Greeks lend me
stateliness as I
proceed toiling up
to the Acropolis,
my Sears and Roebuck
Grecian sandals stepping
in the hot dust,
my drip-dry dress
draping gracefully around
my classic thighs.

Past the Nike temple teaching
delicate strength, past
the maidens of the Erectheum,
my sisters in head-strongness,
I breathe deeply.

Then, the Parthenon,
its columns themselves
a source of sun, an eternal
glow that flows into me.
Gods, am I great!

AT A JAZZ CONCERT: THOUGHTS ON IMMORTALITY
(sonnet)

The clarinet and bass are warm, but chills
run up into my head as soulful strains
remind with throbbing slurs and laughing trills
how life is rich when syncopation reigns.
I've danced to "Closer Walk with Thee" played fast,
I've followed from a graveyard when a band
exulted that their brother-saint had passed:
with jazz the space from grief to joy is spanned.
Tonight I know that I will live again,
and be an everlasting song of jazz.
Just listen, and you'll know I'm living then,
with all intensity the music has.
I know eternity is not too long
for me to dance and sing within a song.

AT DINNER

Voices and glasses clinked
along the table for minute on minute on
till rush of rain attacked,
and thunder
like stones thudding
down in front of me
completing the wall.

AT THE LAST

At the last we seem
a 1930 magazine
angel-like mother and daughter
floating just over reality

The umbilical cord
I had forgotten as I
looked at Giottos
climbed pre-Alps
kissed welders and poets

Now again I see it and reach . . .
Mama, I washed the dishes, Mama . . .
She trails up and up
and filters into the atmosphere.

AUGUST

August heavy-lidded
holds close her wealth,
vines with purple splotches
the drooping grapes heavy as udders,
fat droning flies,
orange-red tomatoes
bursting to the sun.
August smells of oozing heat,
lolls in yellow afternoon
like a spent lover
with no thought of tomorrow.

BALLERINA

We have forgotten to
emerge from our cocoons and
like you (and Adam and Eve)
flutter and skim and,
glorying through air,
light on a moment.

LET ME

This is fun,
but a million years
is long enough
strutting around in
these clothes and these ideas.
Let me be God
for a while,
or else a gorilla.

BETWEEN US LET US STRETCH A STRING

Between us let us stretch a string,
Hold it tightly, keep it taut,
No loosening, laxing, unawaring,
Twanging when we try to pluck it,
But feel the tug in the connection,
Tension-taut and vibrant-live,
Quick to spring and sometimes sing,
Responsive to our touch.

BLUEBERRY PICKING

Sunday
I skipped church
for blueberrying
where I discovered
excuse the expression
God.
Had we walked fields and paths
swinging our buckets
instead of driving
(though the tree-lined curves
were a deja-vu of birth)
I might have recognized It sooner.
It was knee-high in the Queen Anne's lace
as we were crossing to the blueberries.
It was in the silence
of Jean and Carrie.
And then
revealing Itself to anyone who looked
It was five berries
delicate as dawn
pink, lavender, white, pale green, grey-blue
on one startling stem.

PHANTOM
(to Michael G.)

In his red sweater,
with spelling book in hand,
he headed out into
the dark October morning,
letting in a piece of chill
before he closed the door.

By now he must be standing out
by the mailbox and the black-eyed Susans,
kicking pebbles and watching down the road.

Now, they push into sight --
the large dim yellow eyes,
the bulky phantom, its grey-orange aura
filtering the dark.
It hesitates
by the mailbox,
then creeps away.

A CHILD IS

(to Andrew G.)

A child is a person that knows
absolute silence is necessary
to watch a cloud
moving over the moon.

CHRIS

(to Christopher G.)

Chris caught a ladybug
when his daddy went up
to get his Ph.D.
He let it scramble
up and down my closed umbrella.
When they were handing out
the diplomas, he let it go.
"Someday I'll get another ladybug,"
he said.

DANDELION WINE

In December
when I drink the pale wine,
I'll see the dandelions and us
in the windy spring,
pity our hope as we picked blooms
like promises: we'd use them for wine,
you said, to drink at Christmas.
But, like blooms, the promises withered
when you died, and I'll taste the wine alone.

DANDELIONS

When April comes, the meadows, fields,
and vacant lots are all bestarred
with glorifying dandelions.
Sometimes I even see a *yard*
that's bursting out in smiles.
But Dad and neighbors call them *weeds*
and dig them up no matter how
a dandelion-lover pleads.
They say, "No, weeds don't smile at us,
'cause we and weeds can't co-exist";
but if you'll look by our back fence,
you'll see a giggle that Dad missed.

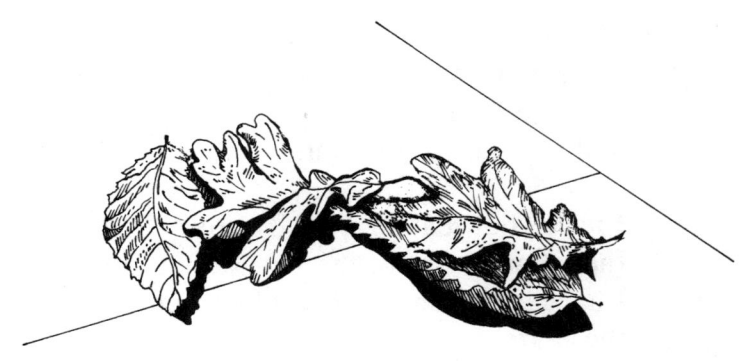

DRY LEAVES

Dry leaves skipping, scuttering
across my path
brown and cracked
they should be dead
but they act alive

always
dry leaves are skipping, scuttering
recollecting
across my path

FATHER

I find, among your papers,
"I have known what it is
to stand with my feet in the mud
and my head in the stars."

I have your leather-bound books
the color of clay of the Patoka bottoms,
I have your pen, mottled black and white:
these are the stars.

But I have none of the mud,
can only hold child-days
of learning farm lore
of cucumber hills with miniature trenches,
of my fingers closing
on a slick thin worm to bait a hook.

And so
mind must tell heart
the precious mix.

THE FIRST WARM WINDY DAY

The first warm windy day
youth in sky-blue denims
scattered on the Student Building steps
watching a pet ocelot,
a circled yellow ocelot
born in Ecuador
to be watched
on the Student Building steps
by youth in sky-blue denims
on the first warm windy day.

I KNEW AN APPLE TREE

I chose the apartment for the apple tree
outside the kitchen window.
I knew the tree when it flushed with blossoms
for one passionate day,
zinging my head like a roller coaster.
I knew the tree when summer richness dotted it
with cool-dipped apples,
young as childhood mornings.
I knew the tree when apples dropped with days,
plunking like the basketball
dribbled by the boy next door.
I knew the tree when the leaves warmed
like hundreds of dallying afternoons
that say "Come be with me."
I knew the tree when winds blew and leaves sailed
and winds blew again,
until only a few leaves shimmered
like violinists' hands in vibrato.
I knew the tree with bare, bony branches
and infinity of loneliness beyond,
but when two squirrels chased up the trunk,
along a branch, bending it low,
and arched to the next tree,
it was as if all outdoors knew Thanksgiving.
I knew the tree when a setting sun
called out a glow from the branches,
and I knew that we were beginning again.

The next day, the sound began.
Buzzing, raving, ranting,
raging, razzing, it broke the day.
At day's end I dared to look.

Humiliated stood the dwarfed trunk,
like a robot with stubby arms.
Nearby lay sliced limbs, neatly bundled, their ends
glaring and naked,
and out by the alley
twigs of new life
stuck out of the garbage cans.

I knew an apple tree.

HI BLUE

Skip blue
Kick blue
Hi blue
like a

dipping flipping high kite blue
like a

classy glassy bottle blue
like a

gleamy dreamy deep lake blue
like a

bolting jolting boxcar blue

Skip blue
Kick blue
Hi blue

IN HONOR OF *TIME* PHOTOGRAPHERS
(1967)

Time now
shows war
in soft hues of
blue eyes
blue tanks
brown leaves
brown guns
coral skies
coral corpses
so that
we understand
that war
is natural.

ITALY

Italy,
hold me in your arms
again, a wanted woman-child,
wrap me in your yellowness,
command me with your warmth, like wine,
repeat to me your ever reply
to life, "Of course."

THE JENNIE ROSE

In the yard next door,
where the old bachelor lives,
a slant of early sun
kisses again the prow
of the white Jennie Rose,
unused and lonely except
for the plaster Virgin Mary
among red plastic roses.

BERGAMO AT SIX O'CLOCK

Day muting to end,
first lights glimmering up in Old Town
as if ghosts have found their souls.
Here in Low Town rain
whispers down "buona sera"
hushing sputters of bikes
and buses' whines;
under nodding black umbrellas,
swirling ones of pink
and green and blue,
the voices tap "buona sera"
and now contrapuntal church bells
call across the piazza
"buona sera."

MAHLER SYMPHONY
(acrostic)

Victoriously Mahler's symphony soars
Above world and words
Like the man with two canes
In the station this morning, creeping
Across the endless floor,
Negotiating every inch. Privately a human
Tortoise soars.

MOM AND DAD

When my mother was a child,
she liked to yell and run wild,
chase a dog down the street,
walk around with bare feet,
ride a tricycle over bumps,
jump the way a rabbit jumps.

When my father was a lad,
he liked to make his sister mad,
had told her it was only fake
when he scared her with a snake,
scraped and scrapped, wore holes in pants,
fed bread and jelly to the ants.

Mom and Dad used to be
fanciful children just like me.

MY DOG

I spoke Human to her,
she spoke Dog to me,
and for years
we understood.
Then one day
on the steps
she always scampered up,
her old legs made her stumble
and her huge brown eyes,
startled, reproachful, asked why
and I could not answer.

MY LATEST POEM

You tease me
with your words
I tease you back
there have been others
but none quite so
titillating as you
you fresh my days
and caress my nights
I am complete again

ONE RAINDROP

Can't I just watch
this one raindrop
reflecting the world
and let the rest go?
Maybe that childhood dream
with stifling rugs
surrounding me,
then the pinpoint
funneling me to itself,
smooth and pure, was
my life-dream.

Maybe the rugged orange,
handed me in Delphi,
with stem and leaf,
can be just enough,
or the child's face
when he said, "What *is* God,
anyway?"
Maybe just
the leaf-shadows in
the kitchen sun,
and forget the in-between.

OPERA AT THE BATHS OF CARACALLA

The hulking ruins like ancient Romans
loom into our lives,
dwarf Aida and her lover defying
dwarfness thrusting out
throbbing throated notes
to join eternity.
Believers for fifty minutes,
we hang on points of stars
above the monumental past replayed.

Then in a flood of lights
we find ourselves
on wooden seats
where fellow men
cry "Coca Cola, caffe"
to earn their pasta
for tomorrow.

OUR YELLOW

Our two halves
never did make a whole, but
I can feel our yellow
like a sprinkle of dandelions
over the world
or a halo around its head
and it makes the world warm.

CAFE

Always Nevada and always
supper-time here,
always a catsup bottle
more familiar than the Tower of Pisa,
always a black-sweatered waitress
mopping table swirls, always
cushioning tones of
"I Can't Stop Loving You"
drifting from somewhere.
I sit alone and watch the door
for Sir Lancelot.

PIAZZA QUIRINALE
(triolet)

The Roman square in noonday sun lay still
and Alessandro gently kissed me there
near two majestic horsemen on the hill.
The Roman square in noonday sun lay still
with pines and us alive alone until
the spirits from the ages filled the air.
The Roman square in noonday sun lay still
and Alessandro gently kissed me there.

QUEEN OF THE MOUNTAIN

Flicked in my face
dropped on my head
flung at my back

It piled
and hardened
I climbed it

Keep off my dung hill

RAIN WHIMSEY

Last night
rain came and whispered
soft secrets to me.
It whispered all the dandelions' names
and how many raindrops in the world.
Suddenly from somewhere
rumbled jumbling thunder,
boasting, celebrating rain
and sun and wind and night and day,
promising, "Always we'll be here."
At last rumble dropped to mumble,
"Remember, remember, remember!"
as the thunder rolled away,
and I could hear the rain again,
whispering the secret
of where the thunder went.

SARAJEVO

1946
In Mrs. Rutledge's history class
we came to 1914. Somehow
the only fact of World War I
that stuck with me was how
it started, the archduke and his wife
killed in Sarajevo.
I slipped the picture into my head,
along with Latin conjugations.

1974
Meriana, dark-haired girl,
my guide in Sarajevo, pointed out
dome-topped Muslim stones
in the cemetery and took me
to the archduke's footprints
marked in the sidewalk.
We had tea in the late afternoon
at a sidewalk cafe
with her father, grey, stalwart, smiling,
handsome regardless of one gold tooth,
fond of Americans.
"I would like," he beamed,
"to travel by train in America
from Charleston to San Francisco."

1992
Each day I study photographs in the news
of Sarajevo, faces amidst
shelling, starving, killing.
I wonder if I would recognize the dark-haired girl,

the handsome man with the gold tooth,
and wish that history would keep out of Sarajevo.

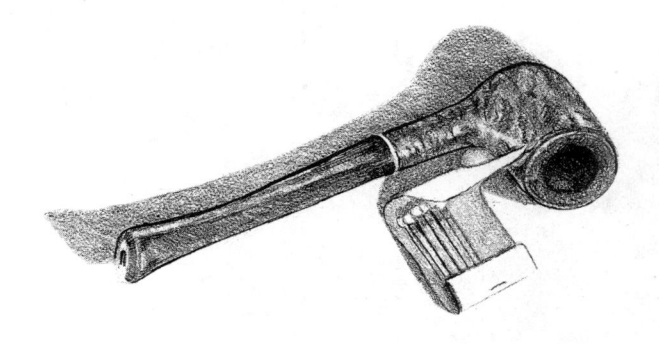

WE TWO

You come with your pipe and your glinting laughter,
I'll come with Frost poems and Fountain jazz,
we'll move in a park of Dr. Zhivago snow,
both of us full of tiny lights,
leaving the world with its truths.

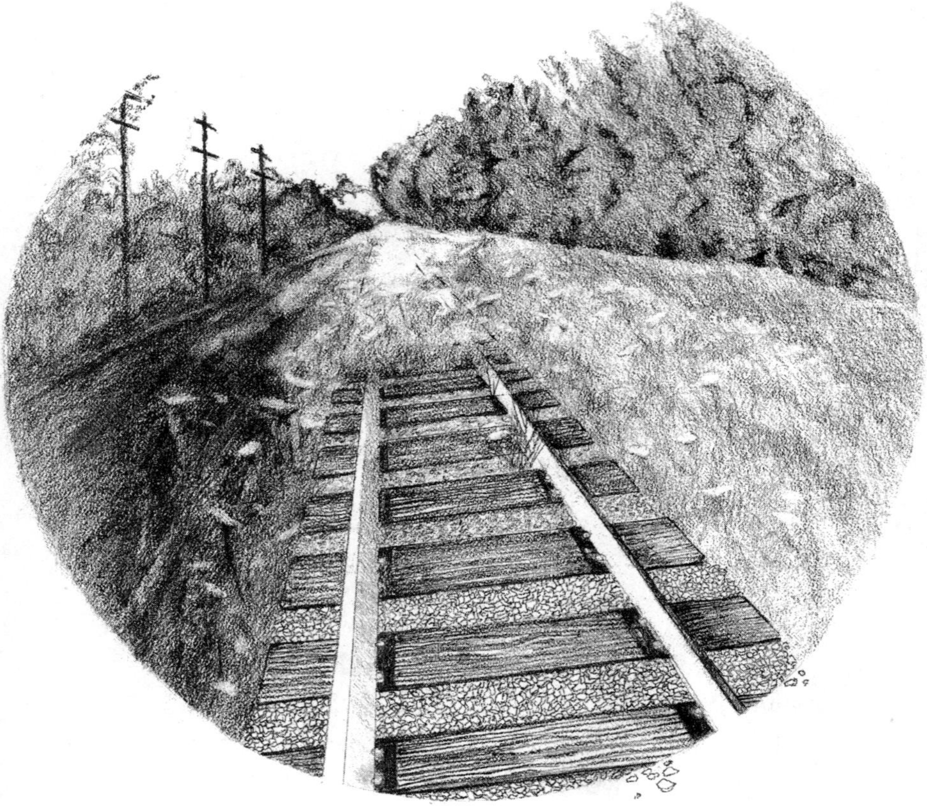

SEEKING

I drive the gravel roads
through the cornfields of my father's youth,
look down the railroad track
he followed to school in town,
feel his way at twilight
down the tree-lined
curving road he drove
from Sunday dates with Mother,
hear him in his brother's voice--
he would sound that way,
search his face in pictures
to see beginnings of the man I knew.
Thus pulling from the nagging world,
I seek a father-womb.

A SIXTEENTH-NOTE REST

My childhood Indian necklace has one blue
discordant bead because
"Only God is perfect"
someone said.
I like that but also I like
Greeks of the Parthenon who
worked with God-like love
on hidden sides of gods.

Now my brother and I sit
on his back porch. He says
"We spent two minutes on one
sixteenth-note rest --
to get it right." He
smiles slightly in the dusk
with nearby oaks and pines holding
back the weakening light.
"Two minutes on one
sixteenth-note rest,
to get it right.
The director said 'It's not
a thirty-second note
not an eighth-note
but a sixteenth-note.'"

Thus my brother reminisces
with a reverence, he
that always says "If you can
show me God then
I'll believe."
Wave lengths of love for a director
who envisioned a perfect sixteenth-note rest
pass in the dark from my brother to me.
We sit still, practicing the silence,
worshipping all who dare to leave
the blue bead out.

RIDING IN THE RAIN

Drizzle
drizzle
soft jazz
jazz
yellow lights gleam
on black pavement
wet
tires smack
I look
at the world
from this womb

THE SIXTH DAY

The bare tree with
Feather twigs in winter --
In my image,
And the constant living sun --
The fourth day's work
Was also good,
And the dolphin of the fifth day
Is smooth and pure and quick.
Now the lion prowls the forest,
Dignified and sure,
Devoted to my image, but man
Is taking long. With his brain
He can maim and he can heal;
He can mock and he can soothe;
But he fears so much
To lose his self that
He cannot be one
With tree and sun, dolphin, lion.
Help, Socrates, Jesus, Ghandi!
Will this sixth day never end?

SILENCE

Silence deafens, echoes
all
voices clamoring,
all
mimicking monotones
crammed, crunching,
all
screams hemorrhaged
until
suddenly blissfully cut
off by the free busy lullaby
of a motorbike.

A SMOOTH BLACK STONE

We padded along the damp
hard brown sand
daring waves to chill
our feet, past the lifeguard,
past the last frolickers,
with the day ending
behind our backs.
He handed me
a smooth black stone,
perfect, with a tiny hole.

Now flat on my palm
it is a stranger, and I know
I should have thrown it far
out into the waves
for another time,
another moment.

SNOW-WHITE AND THE SEVEN DWARFS
(an Epilogue for Cynics)

Sneezy followed Doc's advice about a bad attack;
Sneezy died, and Doc was jailed because he was a
                                                                   quack.
Sleepy looked for more in life and started smoking pot;
life for him was full of dreaming if asleep or not.
Dopey's freedom ended--he was put away for life.
Bashful shed his backward ways and took another's
                                                                     wife.
Grumpy murdered Happy, started smiling his disguise,
living with a pleasant face no one could recognize.

Snow-White fed the poisoned apple to Prince
                                                     Charming's horse,
leading this romantic pair into divorce, of course.

THE THIRTIES: EAST CHICAGO, INDIANA

John Dillinger robbed the First National Bank
one day, lending glamor
to our gutsy hub of steel and oil.

Only a child-person knew it as enchanted--
orange train running through the main street,
headed for Chicago--
grey days a foghorn from the canal
bellowing camaraderie--
Bank Night at the movies with five hundred dollars
going to fat sixth-grader Danny --
little Old World daughters
in tiny earrings
and too-long dresses
jumping rope on the playground --
harbinger of summer,
the knife-sharpener's pushcart
with its dinging bell --
collie's noontime trip
to the railroad-crossing man
with his brown bag lunch --
Miss Davis, librarian,
with twelve silver bracelets on her arms,
yelling "Hello, Cookie!" at each child --
and diamond-sparkles
in the down town sidewalks --
J.D., did you notice?

THIS ROSE PETAL

This rose petal,
fragile and paled,
I must have placed
in this book some year
so as never,
never to forget.

TO THE CYNIC AT CHRISTMAS

To the cynic at Christmas:
All is not lost in the cash register.
We can know
the star
in a candle
awe
for a snow-glistened tree
gifts of kings
in red-wrapped boxes
and worship
in love for each other.

TO YOU, THE RED-HAIRED BOY

To you, the red-haired boy
who pronounced me ugly
at fifteen (I already knew),
leading me to
believe in Don Quixote and the Sphinx
and go looking for them,
thank you.

TOUR GUIDE

The old guide
climbs the bus steps
as he climbs
the years now --
thoughtfully
picking them out --
the bus rolls on.
"Mozart and Shubert and Strauss,"
his voice vibrates
lovingly around the names,
"came often here, to
the Vienna Woods."
He returns down from
eternity and,
removing his spectacles,
wipes his bleary eyes, then
watches the girl in
the front seat as
she crosses her legs.

VIEW FROM 175TH STREET

In my years of looking out this window
with the God's-eye view,
the roofs of mediocre houses
and second-thought garages
have become Edward Hopper slants and slopes
playing off each other
under changing suns and rains.

In the closest tree
a giant squirrel's nest sways high,
but against the distance
tawdry jumbled treetops
are forests of fairy tales
in my old but youthful eyes.

There is a sometimes sky
when western sun rays
remembering raindrops
have touched my east
with Monet light
that filters gold and blue
like tissue paper,
and bare twigs come to life,
and I have caught it all.

Last night when the moon
drew me to the window,
the lights six blocks over on Maple Street

had become an unreachable, mystical mountain
town along the coast of Amalfi.

My windowed masterpiece,
I have made you what you are.

TRUMP

You kept me interested,
it cannot be denied,
in all our arguments,
in all the ways we vied.
At puzzles, chess, and bridge,
you won -- I only tried.
I laughed with you, but when
I told my jokes -- you sighed.
I gasped at autumn leaves --
you smugly classified.
I was awed by music --
you identified.
Any point of history --
you proudly clarified.
Pronunciation errors --
you quickly rectified.
After I had taken
all I could abide,
I played at hard-to-get,
for I was satisfied
that I could win, but no --
you played your trump -- you *died!*

TWO TOURISTS MEET

Across the table
your lean El Greco face,
dark searching eyes,
heavy brows,
shed the joking mask
like a painting restored.
We brought out one by one
our hoarded thoughts,
storm-thoughts,
art-thoughts,
God-thoughts,
then carefully hid them away again.
Good-bye,
Fellow Thunder-lover.

WHO?

The carrot I see, dangling before me.
But the driver --
Apollo, Buddha, God, Quixote?

WYOMING EVENING
(haiku)

Cool and a rainbow
have come to the evening.
The sagebrush is sweet.

Near the cottonwood
the cowboys recite their poems.
Cows move in the field.

The rainbow fades and
the cowboys recite their poems
under a half moon.

ZELDA
(triolet)

Zelda thinks that she's a queen,
With us her lowly peasants.
With rich black fur and jewels of green,
Zelda thinks that she's a queen
Lending to the mundane scene
Sophisticated presence.
Zelda thinks that she's a queen
With us her lowly peasants.

IF IT WEREN'T FOR DANDELIONS

Early I learned a difference
between children and the other people
and it was dandelions.
That was before
red deep-sweet roses surrounded
my father's casket
and before
I stood waist-deep with Richard
in Ann Hathaway's dream-filled garden
and before
Aprils
of driving all alone
to seek out meadows
overflowing with sun-drops.
If it weren't for dandelions
nothing would connect.

WISH

May you run
with songs
at your heel
May you catch
all your balloons
except one
May we meet
wherever
we may go,
Wandering
in Queen Anne's
lace

FOREIGNER

We were talking,
my Pakistanian Moslem friend
and I.
"When I was little,"
I said,
"we used to stick peanut shells on the ends
                                      of our fingers."
"We too,"
he smiled,
"we too."

AMALFI, ITALY

The hydroplane lifted from the water, and we skimmed along smoothly and almost noiselessly. We passed the town of Praiano, its layers of houses with staring windows. Close to Praiano, on a rock jutting out over the water, was one of the various round stone watchtowers which accentuate the Amalfi coastline on the Tyrrhenian Sea. They used to be lookout towers against the Saracens in medieval days, when Amalfi was an independent maritime republic.

Now I could see Amalfi's many tiers of houses and lemon groves coming into view, with the Capachin convent, now used as a hotel, high on a mountain above all else.

It was just for the experience that I had chosen the hydroplane today for the ten-minute trip between Positano and Amalfi. Always before when I had traveled anywhere along the Amalfi coastline, which stretches from Sorrento to Salerno, I had traveled by bus.

On my first two bus trips along the drive several years before, I knew that I had never had any other spiritual experience to equal this: the ancient, solid, towering mountain walls stark and stern; the dramatic juts, edges, ridges, jags; the more friendly creases, slopes, and terraces of wild brush and wild flowers, evergreens, grape vines, lemon and fig and olive groves; the occasional little white or yellow house or group of houses in Moorish style, clinging impertinently to the mountainside; the constantly winding road; below the road more terraces, trees, little houses; and finally the blue, blue Tyrrhenian Sea. Looking ahead of the bus or backward, one can see all levels at once, as the coastline is that irregular.

After those two bus trips, I had returned other years to spend time in Amalfi, then Ravello, farther up in the mountains, this time Positano.

Now our hydroplane was docking at Amalfi, where I planned to spend the day. A white-haired man, short, his fat belly pushing out his white tee-shirt, briskly tied the vessel.

The water here at Amalfi's shore was lively with rowboats, motorboats, and bobbing heads of swimmers; and the sounds of motors and yells pierced the air. Beyond the narrow beach ran a street busy with several buses and many taxis and Fiats. A travel agency, a cafe, a shop with post cards and little sculpture reproductions gave an air of tourism to even the bank, the pharmacy, and the fruit shop.

I left this street fronting the sea. A passageway hardly deserving to be called a street led to the main piazza of the town. The two buildings that flanked the passageway were joined by an arch overhead, probably actually a room or a hallway.

A small car was inching through the passageway, past a sandal stall which took up part of the street, past two parked motorbikes, and past pedestrians, several of whom crossed in front of the car even though it honked frequently. Just before the break out onto the piazza, was a butcher shop. Inside and out, it was all glass, steel, and white marble, contrasting with other buildings older and more colorful, and as startling as a block of ice would be in a rock garden. There was a big bouquet of pink roses in the front window, however, beside the pink carcass of half a cow.

Out in the piazza, people moved in and out of shops, some crossed the piazza, and others sat at the outdoor tables of a cafe. Across from me was the cathedral at the top of a tall, wide flight of stairs. It is Sicilian-Arabic in style, with a stone facade of black and white geometric designs and golden, glinting mosaics. I passed by the small fountain of the piazza and climbed the steps to the cathdral. Three years before, I had visited the cathedral, but I wanted to see the lovely cloisters again.

The criss-cross design above the Romanesque columns in the cloisters give a combined lacy and sturdy impression. I was pained again, however, by the defacement of the walls and columns that had shocked me before -- mostly people's initials.

Descending to the piazza, I decided that for lunch, instead of going to a restaurant or buying only a couple of bananas to eat on the street, I would buy some picnic things, even though I was alone. I went about spotting shops where I would later buy various items, thus planning my menu.

It was good to have a purpose in mingling with the other busy people. Yelling and honking jabbed all around me. The sound of beach clogs and the strong smell of fish for sale in front of every fifth shop or so were constant reminders of the nearby sea.

Spying a *latteria*, I wondered if they would have small cartons of milk as well as the usual liter bottles. I parted the red, green, and blue plastic strips hanging in the doorway and entered. I found that they carried half-liter cartons, some cheeses, and even rolls. Outside another shop I spotted some miniature *fiascos* of Chianti, just the thing to add to the roll and goat's milk cheese for an Italian picnic although the milk would be an unorthodox touch.

Around twelve-thirty I retraced my steps, this time buying. A few shops were beginning to close for siesta, and the owners were pulling down the wood-slatted coverings over their doorways.

Where to eat? I could not remember if there was a place nearby that would be more pastoral than these surroundings. I explored several streets that led away from the piazza. To follow those in one direction, I needed to climb steps. Residences and more shops lined all the streets and the tiny piazzas that frequently interrupted the streets. I did not really want to sit outside someone's house to eat my lunch, although I had once done that on Mykonos.

Finally I followed a main street, Via Genova, out of the main piazza, in the direction of the old paper mill that I remembered. Since nothing looked like a picnic site, I settled down on a curb across from some yellow concrete apartment houses and began to unpack my lunch.

A man in a natty brown jacket approached on a motorcycle and stopped near me. Evidently he lived nearby, and I had his usual parking place. He asked me to move a little farther along the curb. I decided to try to find a place farther from the center and moved on up the street, which was narrowing to a path. I passed, on my right, yellow, cream, and pink houses with pots of flowers on their balconies.

Some balconies now had green canvas shades drawn out over them against the sun. I had been noticing a stream on my left, and now I came to the little white-washed building that was the paper mill. Again, as three years before, it seemed secretive and rather uninviting, huddled against a bluff and with no signs of life except for a rumbling sound coming out of the open door.

Behind the mill was a three-foot wall bordering the stream. Here I perched and ate, glad to be in a rather secluded place with the running water and the squeaking mill wheel.

I thought of the travel article in a Chicago newspaper in which the writer had said that she had visited this mill. When I had been here before, I had seen nothing to encourage me to enter. A little resentfully I dwelt on how newspaper writers can get in anywhere.

When I had finished eating, I gathered up the carton, the bottle, and the cheese rinds into the paper that the cheese had come in. I walked around to the front of the mill and peered through the doorway. The inside looked dim and smelled musty. The squeaks and swishes sounded as old as the place looked.

A man emerged from the recesses. He wore a grey shirt and trousers. His hair was thinning in front; a front tooth was missing; his eyes were very watchful but soft, his manner diffident.

"Come in," he said in Italian.

"May I see?" I asked.

"*Si. Entri.*"

The main part of the building was only as large as an average living-room, dining-room area. I saw heaps of used carton boxes in several places. "Do you use these boxes to make paper?" I asked in my passable Italian.

"*Si.*" He began to lead me farther in, past machinery. "I ate my meal outside," I said. I displayed my package and laughed. "May I throw this someplace?"

He took it from me and threw it in among some carton boxes. I knew that he had been able to feel the bottle among it, but he did not seem to be particular about the quality of the trash. I wondered what the bottle and the cheese rind would do to the paper-making process.

We now stood by a vat in which an acrid-smelling, grey- colored mush of cartons was disintegrating. We passed along toward the rollers. The floor here was sloping and a little slimy, and he put his hand under one of my elbows. He explained the process, and I asked for clarification whenever he used an unfamiliar Italian word. The mill uses an ancient method, including hand- beating the paper with a wooden block.

The little tour was finished, and we stood now near the door.

"Are you staying in Amalfi?" he asked.

"No, Positano."

"I would like to show you Amalfi."

"Oh, no, *grazie*. I have been here before, and I have walked much in Amalfi."

"We could walk together this evening."

"No, *grazie*. I am returning to Positano this afternoon. I should go now. Thank you for permitting me to visit."

He looked at me solemnly. Then he asked me to sit on a straight-backed chair and wait a few minutes. He hurried out the door and went to an adjacent building. When he returned, he presented me with two envelopes which said in Italian, "Hand-made paper of Amalfi" and which were filled with stationery and matching envelopes. The paper was a light cream color, rich and beautiful, the mill's best grade. The edges were daintily jagged, and there were watermarks of a design and the word *Amalfi*.

I thanked him as profusely, I hoped, as an Italian would have, we shook hands, and I left the mill, no longer jealous of newspaper writers.

I retraced my steps toward the town center. It was hot mid-afternoon; I kept thinking of lemonade. One little cafe had six small tables outside, covered with white tablecloths. I sat down, and a little boy around ten years of age took my order. He wore a long-sleeved white shirt and black knee-length pants. Unsmilingly business-like, he quickly turned away and entered the cafe.

Another boy around the same size and dressed in the same way was taking an order at another table. Both boys continued briskly moving about and speaking abruptly to each other concerning their work.

While I drank my lemonade, a slightly bigger boy approached on a bicycle and rode it between two tables up to the building. He smiled teasingly. The boy who was my waiter shouted at him angrily, but to no avail. My boy waiter then reached for a broom inside the door and raised it threateningly. The boy drove his bicycle between other tables and then left. My boy glanced my way. His look told of his embarrassment at being a man of business and yet being ineffectual in such a situation.

When I paid my waiter, I pointed to the other boy waiting on tables and asked, "Is he your brother?"

"*Si*."

"May I take a picture of you and your brother?"

"*Si*." Smiling now, he told his brother. They stood together and put their arms around each other's shoulders. When I had finished, my boy said, "*Per favore*, send me a copy of the picture." I agreed, and he rushed into the cafe, returning shortly with a paper with his name and address.

A short time before four I wandered in the direction of the bay, to the huge parking lot for the buses that run between the towns along the coast. In the maze of buses I found the one that would go through Positano, and boarded.

Almost all Italian buses that I have ever seen have looked new. This one had blue seats covered with grey cloths. I looked toward the front to check the dashboard. Yes, there was a small vase with a fresh yellow flower.

More people climbed on, and we eventually started. The bus driver's "friend," as Italian workers always refer to a fellow worker, came back and collected our fares, then returned to his seat opposite the driver. We charged along the narrow road, now hugging a mountainside, now pushing around a curve, with our horn braying like a donkey and all of us holding on to the seats before us so as not to tilt out of our seats, now almost hanging out over the seaward edge of the road and trees, now plunging through a tunnel with red, black, and white posters flashing by -- *Cinzano, La Traviata, Coca Cola*. But as usual, the scenes were even more breath-taking than the ride.

Occasionally we had to slow down to strain around a double curve. On the other side of Praiano we came upon a line of eight cars at a standstill. The source of trouble was out of view around a curve of mountain, but we could see that cars were lined up also in the other direction.

After we had waited a few minutes, the bus driver's friend got off and sauntered ahead to look around the curve. A few other men were leaving their cars to see what the trouble was. A few disappeared around the curve while the others stayed within our view, talking to each other and gesticulating widely. Some were laughing. Finally our driver left to join a small group of the men.

After an additional ten-minute wait, there was a general shifting among the men down the road, and our driver's friend seemed to be giving directions with his arms to a vehicle which was still out of our sight. Men began returning to their cars, and our driver came. The vehicle rounded the curve. It was a truck.

Many of us had been standing in the aisle watching the activity, and we could look down onto the bed of the truck as it passed and could see that it held huge, perhaps three-foot-high *fiascos* of wine. In the truck cab, the two men, brown, creased, thin, looked ahead stoically.

Our driver's friend and other drivers had not been in a hurry to return to their cars because behind the truck was a bus, which was constantly hindered by the truck's progress, and which was having a few problems of its own. Now, for instance, it was going to have difficulty passing our bus. Our driver's friend decided that our bus could help by moving back and a little closer to the mountain wall.

He walked to the back of our bus and began giving the customary signals to the driver by pounding on the bus -- two quick raps for "continue," one loud one for "stop." Meanwhile, the other bus was inching by. The passengers on it and we on our bus smiled broadly at each other across the few feet that separated us. When the two buses were finally clear of each other, passengers around me cheered the two drivers -- "*Bravi! Bravi!*"

We continued then to Positano.

BERGAMO, ITALY

In a week I was going to give an American teen-age type supper for six Italian teen-agers. They were my students in the advanced English class at the Liceo Classico in Bergamo. The only problem I could foresee concerning the supper was the hamburger buns. I asked Vittoria, whose apartment I shared, if a bakery would try to make some according to my description. She assured me that they would.

I cut a cardboard circle the size of a bun, and, that afternoon, went to the bakery on Via Manzoni. There I handed over the cardboard circle, indicated the appropriate thickness with my fingers, and emphasized, "*Molto morbidi,*" -- very soft.

"*Si, si,*" two of the sales people said.

The following Saturday I would pick up the buns.

Now I walked to the small grocery store in the next block to get cokes. Cokes came only singly, not in cartons; and so I would need to buy a few at a time whenever I was in the center of town.

The grocery store was next to a shop that fascinated me, one which sold only rope. Through the open door one could see some of the coils of rope piled on the floor -- all sizes of rope. I could see the owner, dressed in a bright blue business suit, and several customers.

The little grocery store was a self-service one, but not nearly as far up the American razzle-dazzle supermarket line as the big Upim store. There was hardly any attempt at attractive displays, and the small amounts of all items made it look as if children were playing store. For example, on one table were the eggs, by two's, three's, and four's, tied in little nets.

I bought four cokes, took my string bag from my purse, and put them into it.

Whenever I had been out to dinner and had to wait by myself at the bus stop, with the streets practically deserted and nothing to watch, I had to sing all the stanzas of "On Top of Old Smoky" to keep myself company.

Now, in the daytime, with three other people waiting for busses, I found the scene entertaining. Motor bikes zipped along the street, sounding gritty and energetic. Women, in short dresses and dress shoes, rode behind their men, their arms circling the men's waists. Fiats, slightly larger than the motor bikes, whizzed by, braking suddenly at the stop light. Bicycles zigzagged about their business. Two men on bicycles, not in such a hurry, rode abreast, one arm of each extended to rest on the other's shoulder.

It was around five o'clock. In an hour would start the daily *passeggiatta*, especially on the main street, with swarms of people strolling arm in arm, greeting friends, eying everyone's clothes. With the weather mild, it being the last of April, many were walking leisurely even now, an hour early, and on this lesser street.

A short, chunky man waiting for a bus asked me in Italian if I were waiting for number two.

"*No,*" I said, "*Numero tre.*"

His look told me that he was deciding that I was foreign. I was a little disappointed since during the year, I had been mistaken more and more frequently for an Italian. "Do you live in Bergamo?"

"*Si.*"

"How do you like Bergamo?" There were kind crinkles next to his eyes.

"*Molto bene.*"

"Would you like to take a *passeggiatta?*"

"*No, grazie.*"

When the number three came, we nodded and said, "*Buona sera,*" and I climbed on the back of the bus. I gave my ticket to the man sitting at the rear and moved up to a seat.

Only a few other passengers were on the bus. Even though there were many empty seats, several riders stood in the aisle, dipping their heads slightly to look out the windows. They clung tightly to the backs of seats as the bus raced a short distance, screeched to a stop, lurched, raced, screeched, lurched. And so I was jerked homeward.

Whenever I was in the center of town during the next week, I bought more cokes or potato chips, which came only in small bags.

Once, when I was in the big Upim store, I found a mustard and relish mixture, which I bought for the hamburgers. Upim was a strange combination of the usual Italian surprises and a little American stodginess, including checkout counters, which tried to force Italians into uncharacteristic queues. Pervading over all was the constant blaring record of "Speedy Gonzales,"

81

which, I had been told, was also always played in the Upim stores as far south as Sicily.

On Friday, the day before my party, I was going out to get the meat. I checked with Vittoria to see that I had the right words for "ground beef" and that I was estimating correctly the number of *etti* I should get.

Vittoria was old enough to be my mother, but we were good friends, having lived together since January.

She widened her serious eyes as she said, "Tell him that you are going to eat it raw, or he will give you much fat."

"Really?" I grinned.

"*Si, si, si.*" Her eyes got even wider.

I went to my bedroom to get ready. From my window I saw that it looked like rain. I looked across at *Città Alta*, the Upper Town of Bergamo, also called the old town. It is located on one of the little foothills of the pre-Alps. I loved its face, with its centuries-old yellow buildings jumbled in the distance. When I was out in the lower town, *Città Alta* would draw my eyes up to it as if it were a shrine. Every day from my bedroom I would watch the moods of *Città Alta* change in the different light. One day would be so clear that every angle of every house would stand out, and also every ledge on the cultivated terraces leading up. At another time, with the afternoon sun on it, it became mellow and misty. On another day it might be almost completely covered by fog. Another time rain would bring out the green green of the terraces. This morning, before rain, the ominous light of the sky brought out the yellow of the buildings.

I found my umbrella and went out. It was warm and not yet raining, and so I walked to the butcher shop in the town center.

Only the butcher was in the shop, a man with nonchalant, amused eyes, and a stereotype Italian moustache. "*Buon giorno.*"

"*Buon giorno.*"

"*Dica, signorina.*" (*Dica* is *tell*. I had learned not to be startled by this abrupt command of shopkeepers.)

"I would like eleven *etti* of ground beef," I said. I had doubted, before this moment, that I would have the nerve to say that I was going to eat it raw; and I found that I did not.

The butcher surprised me, however. "Are you going to eat it raw?" he asked.

"*Sì*," I said. I was grateful for his generous question.

With my package of meat in my string bag, I turned to leave. "*Buon giorno,*" said the butcher.

"*Buon giorno.*"

Before leaving the center, I stopped at a *latteria* for a little rest and a glass of milk. I sat at one of the two little tables where I could look out the open doorway and watch people. A bus with passengers in the aisle went jerking by like a giant hiccup.

It began to rain before I left the *latteria*. The shopkeeper and I exchanged "*Buon giorno's,*" and I stepped out, raising my umbrella. The sidewalks were bobbing with umbrellas, big black ones and garden-colored ones.

The policeman who always stood on a platform with a little roof over him in the center of a main intersection was dressed today in an elegant black rain cape. He wore his usual helmet and white gloves and cuffs; and as usual, his graceful movements of arms, hands, and fingers were a pleasure to watch.

While I waited a few minutes for my bus, a couple of bicycles passed, ridden by young men holding umbrellas. A new spectacle was a man in a business suit, smoking a cigar, holding his umbrella, and riding his bicycle.

The next day, the day of my supper party, I picked up the hamburger buns. They were, indeed, the right size, but the consistency was quite heavy and dense. Oh, well. *Non importa.*

That evening the two boys and four girls all arrived at the apartment around seven o'clock, but by two's, as they always sat in class. They had brought me a decorated tin box of chocolates, a work of art from one of the delightful candy shops. Vittoria briefly helped me greet them in the entry hall and then went to her room, having already eaten.

My guests moved into the living room. In Italy, as I had been informed during my orientation period, there is traditionally more of a social gap between students and instructors than in the States. But Italian young people are self-assured and charming, and these students, at least the girls, did not show signs of being uncomfortable.

Luisa and Angela were slim, lissome, giggly girls with long brown hair, who looked like young Italian movie stars.

Georgio, stocky, calm, with a pleasant slow smile, was a contrast to the other boy, Fabrizio. Fabrizio was slim and had squinted, laughing eyes and almost a constant wide smile. He seemed always on the point of making a quick move or bursting into laughter.

Claudia was a solid-looking girl with short dark hair. Her very straight posture and seriousness gave her a dignified bearing. One time in class something was said about religion in the States and about my being a Protestant. Claudia asked me if I had been attending church in Bergamo. She was very concerned when I answered no, and said, "But I think that there is a little Protestant church on Via XXIV Maggio, near the San Marco Hotel."

Laura looked like a grave pixie. Her short, rich-brown ringlets framed a round freckled face and big, serious eyes. She held her head slightly forward, giving the appearance of deference.

I went to the kitchen, leaving them with the music of my records of "Porgy and Bess" and "The King and I." We had been speaking English, but of course they now began in Italian. Their knowledge of English was good, and they were not embarrassed about using it, but they spoke haltingly and with heavy accents. It had been a unique experience for me the day that we had read orally a J.D. Salinger story with profane dialogue.

I served the supper buffet style, off of Vittoria's tea cart in the living room. As they were preparing their

85

hamburgers with relish, I told them that they must add onion also, or they still would not know a true American hamburger; but I could not induce them to do so.

They took their first bites, and Fabrizio, standing in the middle of the room, announced, "*E buono!*" They all enjoyed the hamburgers.

Knowing that there were no marshmallows in Italy, I had previously arranged for someone at home to send me a bag. I toasted them over a stove burner and offered them. The others waited and joked while they watched Claudia cautiously try hers. After she had closed her teeth on it, she slowly pulled her teeth apart with a surprised look, and they all laughed.

Around nine o'clock, when they were leaving, Vittoria came out to say good-bye. They all shook hands with us.

Their *grazie's* continued out into the hall.

After I had finished washing the dishes, I went to bed. The bell in the tower in *Cittá Alta* was sounding. In Venetian times, when the four huge stone gates of the wall surrounding *Cittá Alta* were closed every night at ten o'clock, the bell was rung a hundred times as a warning that they were closing. Although the gates now remain open, the tradition of the bell-ringing has been broken only one night since then -- a night during the second World War.

I lost count somewhere after eighty.

ABOUT THE AUTHOR

Dona Lu Goldman has won awards for poetry. Some of her work has appeared in Bitterroot, Skylark, and Aspect. She taught English under a Fulbright grant in Bergamo, Italy for one year. She says anything else worth knowing about her can be learned from her poems.